Farrar Straus Giroux
New York

KURT CYRUS

Published simultaneously in Canada by HarperCollins*CanadaLtd*
Color separations by Prestige Graphics
Printed and bound in the United States of America by Berryville Graphics
Designed by Lilian Rosenstreich
First edition, 1997

Library of Congress Cataloging-in-Publication Data
Cyrus, Kurt
Tangle Town / Kurt Cyrus
p.   cm.
[1. Cows—Fiction.   2. City and town life—Fiction.]   I. Title.
PZ7.C9973Tan   1997   [E]—dc20   96-24269   CIP   AC

The mayor of Tangle Town was having a bad
morning. "What's wrong with this crazy door?"
he growled, pushing as hard as he could.

A passing policeman heard the noise.
"Are you okay in there?" he asked.
The mayor shouted back, "No! I'm
getting blisters! Plenty of them!"

"Blasters?" the policeman muttered. Then he announced: "We need blasters! Twenty of them!"

"Twenty?" said a man. "That's every plasterer in the city."

"Disaster in the city!" somebody cried.

It was a typical day in Tangle Town.

High on a nearby hill, Roxy Toppler was milking the cows. "Okay, Mosey," she said. "It's your turn now. Mosey?"

She gave a sharp whistle. "Mosey! Come back here."

Mosey looked around. Then her tail waved goodbye.

Mosey knew she needed milking. But this cow had wandering feet, and some days they just couldn't be stopped.

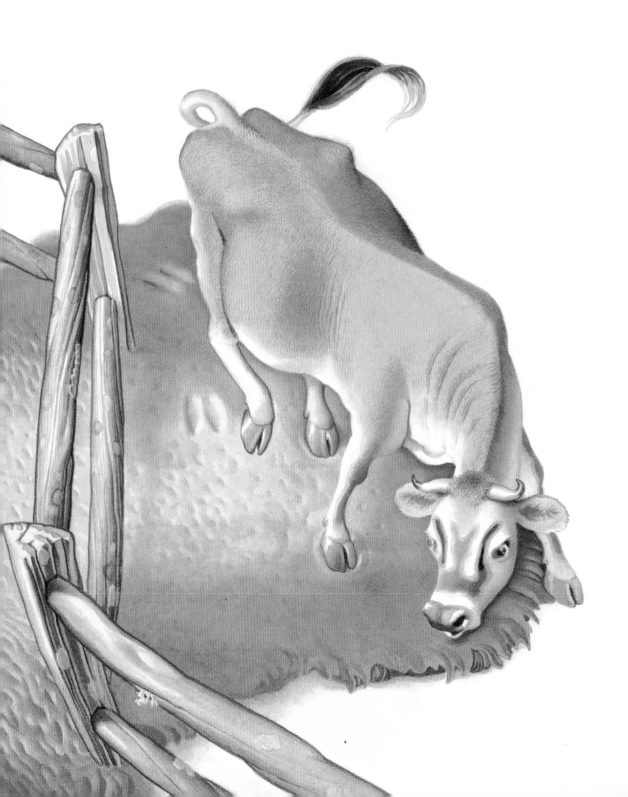

So Roxy got plenty of practice rounding up cattle: "Mo-seeeey! Eeee-yip! Yoo-hoooo, hey, Mosey!"

But today's roundup would be different. "Yikes!" Roxy blurted. "Mosey's made tracks to Tangle Town."

In a hurry, she propped up the fence—just enough to fool the other cows.

Then down the hill she ran.

In the streets of Tangle Town, sirens were wailing. Horns were honking. People were shouting: "Disaster! Disaster!"

"What's going on?" Roxy asked.

"The mayor!"—"The mayor got
blistered!"—"Plastered!"—"Blasted to bits
by twenty twisters!"—"Big, big disaster!"

"Please let me through!" Roxy cried. "I have to catch my cow, and fix my fence!"

"Fix muffins?" someone yelled. "At a time like this? The blasters are coming!" And the confusion just grew worse.

Wow, thought Roxy. *It's just like a stampede of scared cows!* And before she knew it, Roxy's barnyard instincts took over.

First, Roxy whistled her cow whistle, sharp and piercing. The stampeding mob jumped back in surprise.

Then—"Hee-yah! Yah!"—

—the roundup began! "Yip! Yaw!" yelled Roxy, doing what she did best. "Now we're getting somewhere."

She herded the crowd along Zigzag Avenue, up Overtwist Alley, and around Upper Underloop Lane.

"Move along there! Push on through! Eee-yip! Where's that cow?"

Somewhere down around Roundabout
Turnaround, Mosey's wandering feet were
getting a little mixed up.

Whichever way they went, they kept bringing
her back to the Bigtwist Pretzel Mill, where all
the streets of Tangle Town meet.

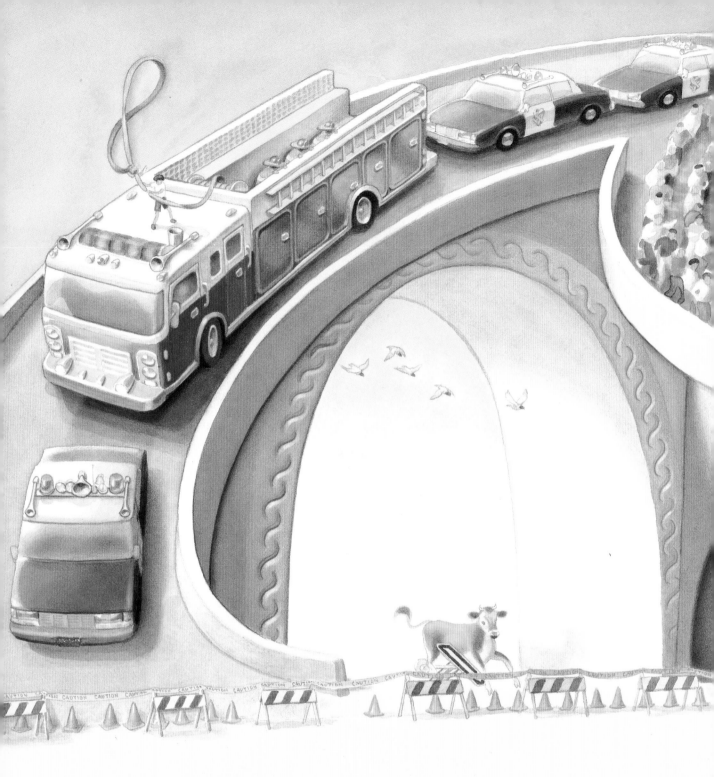

"Here she comes!" hollered Roxy, twirling the fire hose like a lasso. "Head 'er off at the blasting zone. Fence 'er in. Yip! Yip!"

Flash! Boom! The sky filled with pretzels as the No. 20 bin at the Bigtwist Pretzel Mill was blown into tiny bits.

"Hurrah!" cheered the blasters. "We've done it. Just what the mayor ordered."

It was all too much for Mosey. She pushed through the nearest door . . .

. . . and into the office of the mayor. He was sitting there, nursing his blisters in a mustard plaster. "I'm saved!" said the mayor.

"Mmmmooooo," said Mosey.

Before the smoke and dust had cleared, people were going back to their business. Roxy milked. Sweepers swept. Policemen policed, as if nothing unusual had happened. It had just been one of those days . . .

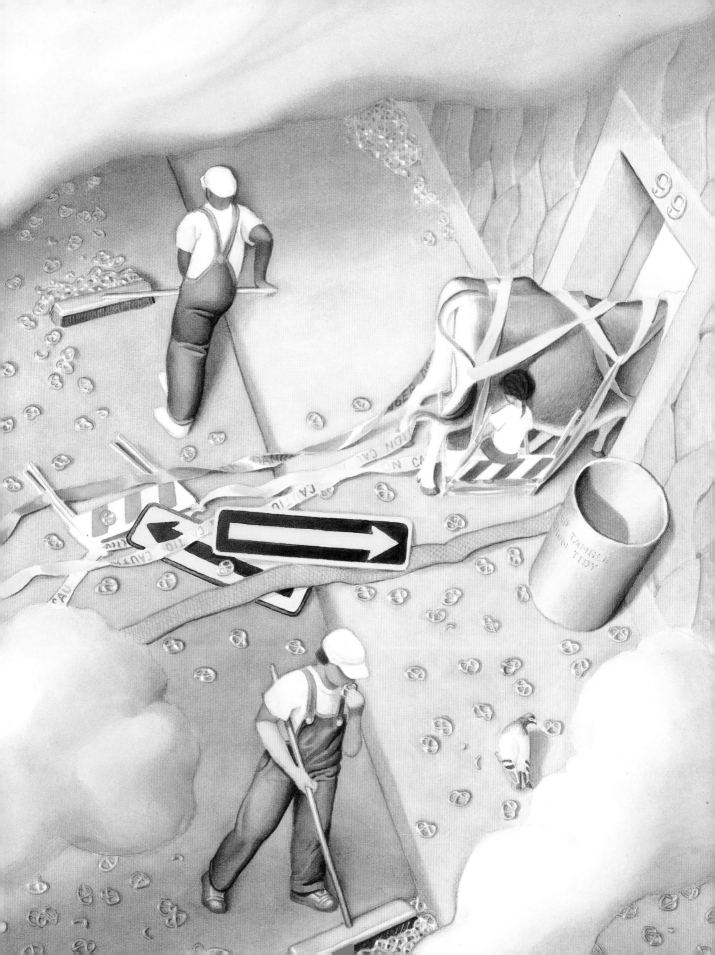

. . . a typical day in Tangle Town.
"What's wrong with this crazy
chair?" growled the mayor.